Baby Billy

Written by Jillian Powell

Illustrated by Helen Flook

Collins

Who's in this story?

Listen and say

Mum

Eve

Billy

Dad

This is Eve. And this is her baby brother, Billy.

Eve and Billy like breakfast.

Mum says, "Oh, Billy! What are you doing?"

Eve likes holding Billy.
But what does Billy like?

Billy likes holding Eve's nose.

Eve likes putting Billy in clean clothes.
But what does Billy like?

Billy likes getting his clothes dirty.
Dad says, "Oh, Billy! What are you doing?"

9

Eve likes feeding Billy some banana.
But what does Billy like?

Billy likes throwing banana on the floor.

Oh, Billy!

11

Eve likes playing with Billy.
But what does Billy like?

Billy likes pushing toys.

Eve likes showing Billy how to draw.
But what does Billy like?

Billy likes drawing on the wall.

Eve likes giving Billy a bath.
But what does Billy like?

Billy likes kicking the water.

Eve likes listening to a story.
But what does Billy like?

Billy likes cuddling Dad.

But what does Billy like doing at the end of the day?

Billy likes sleeping.

Then Mum, Dad and Eve like sleeping, too.

Sleep well, Baby Billy!

Picture dictionary

Listen and repeat

cuddle   draw   feed

kick   play

push   show   throw

1 Look and order the story

2 Listen and say

Collins

Published by Collins
An imprint of HarperCollins*Publishers*
Westerhill Road
Bishopbriggs
Glasgow
G64 2QT

HarperCollins*Publishers*
1st Floor, Watermarque Building
Ringsend Road
Dublin 4
Ireland

William Collins' dream of knowledge for all began with the publication of his first book in 1819.

A self-educated mill worker, he not only enriched millions of lives, but also founded a flourishing publishing house. Today, staying true to this spirit, Collins books are packed with inspiration, innovation and practical expertise. They place you at the centre of a world of possibility and give you exactly what you need to explore it.

© HarperCollins*Publishers* Limited 2020

10 9 8 7 6 5 4 3 2

ISBN 978-0-00-839703-6

Collins® and COBUILD® are registered trademarks of HarperCollins*Publishers* Limited

www.collins.co.uk/elt

British Library Cataloguing in Publication Data

A catalogue record for this publication is available from the British Library.

Author: Jillian Powell
Illustrator: Helen Flook (Beehive)
Series editor: Rebecca Adlard
Publishing manager: Lisa Todd
Product managers: Jennifer Hall and Caroline Green
In-house editor: Alma Puts Keren
Project manager: Emily Hooton
Editor: Tessie Papadopoulou-Dalton
Proofreaders: Natalie Murray and Michael Lamb
Cover designer: Kevin Robbins
Typesetter: 2Hoots Publishing Services Ltd
Audio produced by id audio, London
Reading guide author: Emma Wilkinson
Production controller: Rachel Weaver
Printed and bound by: GPS Group, Slovenia

MIX
Paper from
responsible sources
FSC™ C007454

This book is produced from independently certified FSC™ paper to ensure responsible forest management.

For more information visit: **www.harpercollins.co.uk/green**

Download the audio for this book and a reading guide for parents and teachers at www.collins.co.uk/839703